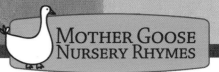

Bedtime

with

MOTHER GOOSE

Compiled by Stephanie Hedlund
Illustrated by Jeremy Tugeau

visit us at www.abdopublishing.com

Published by Magic Wagon, a division of the ABDO Group, 8000 West 78th Street, Edina, Minnesota 55439. Copyright © 2011 by Abdo Consulting Group, Inc. International copyrights reserved in all countries. All rights reserved. No part of this book may be reproduced in any form without written permission from the publisher.

Looking Glass Library™ is a trademark and logo of Magic Wagon.

Printed in the United States of America, North Mankato, Minnesota.
102010
012011
This book contains at least 10% recycled materials.

Compiled by Stephanie Hedlund
Illustrations by Jeremy Tugeau
Edited by Rochelle Baltzer
Cover and interior layout and design by Abbey Fitzgerald

Library of Congress Cataloging-in-Publication Data

Bedtime with Mother Goose / compiled by Stephanie Hedlund ; illustrated by Jeremy Tugeau.
    v. cm. -- (Mother Goose nursery rhymes)
  Contents: Nursery rhymes about bedtime -- As I was going out one day -- It's raining, it's pouring -- Wee Willie Winkie -- Boys and girls, come out to play -- Come, let's to bed -- Diddle, diddle, dumpling -- Early to bed -- Go to bed late -- Good night, sleep tight -- Sleep, baby, sleep -- Hush, little baby -- Little Boy Blue -- Rock-a-bye baby.
  ISBN 978-1-61641-143-5
  1. Nursery rhymes. 2. Bedtime--Juvenile poetry. 3. Children's poetry. [1. Nursery rhymes. 2. Bedtime--Poetry.] I. Hedlund, Stephanie F., 1977- II. Tugeau, Jeremy, ill. III. Mother Goose.
  PZ8.3.B39199 2011
  398.8 [E]--dc22
                    2010024695

Contents

Nursery Rhymes
About Bedtime

Since early days, people have created rhymes to teach and entertain children. Since they were often said in a nursery, they became known as nursery rhymes. In the 1700s, these nursery rhymes were collected and published to share with parents and other adults.

Some of these collections were named after Mother Goose. Mother Goose didn't actually exist, but there are many stories about who she could be. Her rhymes were so popular, people began using *Mother Goose rhymes* to refer to most nursery rhymes.

Since the 1600s, nursery rhymes have come from many sources. The meanings of the rhymes have been lost, but they are an important form of folk language. Nursery rhymes about sleep have long been used to calm children before bed.

As I was going out one day,

My head fell off and rolled away.

But when I saw that it was gone,

I picked it up and put it on.

And when I went into the street,

A fellow cried, "Look at your feet!"

I looked at them and sadly said,

"I've left them both asleep in bed!"

It's Raining, It's Pouring

It's raining, it's pouring,

The old man is snoring;

He got into bed

And bumped his head

And couldn't get up in the morning.

Wee Willie Winkie

Wee Willie Winkie runs through the town,

Upstairs and downstairs in his nightgown,

Rapping at the window, crying through the lock

Are the children all in bed, for now it's eight o'clock?

Boys and Girls, Come Out to Play

Boys and girls, come out to play,

The moon doth shine as bright as day;

Leave your supper and leave your sleep,

And meet your playfellows in the street;

Come with a whoop and come with a call,

Come with goodwill, or not at all.

Up the ladder and down the wall,

A halfpenny roll will serve us all.

You find milk and I'll find flour,

And we'll have a pudding in half an hour.

Come, Let's to Bed

Come, let's to bed,
Says Sleepy-head;
Sit up awhile, says Slow;
Hang on the pot,
Says Greedy-gut,
We'll sup before we go.

To bed, to bed,
Cried Sleepy-head,
But all the rest said No!
It is morning now;
You must milk the cow,
And tomorrow to bed we go.

Diddle, Diddle, Dumpling

Diddle, diddle, dumpling, my son John,

Went to bed with his trousers on;

One shoe off, and one shoe on,

Diddle, diddle, dumpling, my son John.

17

Early to Bed

The cock crows in the morn
To tell us to rise,
And he that lies late
Will never be wise:

For early to bed
And early to rise
Is the way to be healthy
And wealthy and wise.

Go to Bed Late

Go to bed late,

Stay very small;

Go to bed early,

Grow very tall.

Good Night, Sleep Tight

Good night, sleep tight,
Don't let the bedbugs bite.

Sleep, Baby, Sleep

Sleep, baby, sleep,
Thy father guards the sheep;
Thy mother shakes the dreamland tree
And from it fall sweet dreams for thee,
Sleep, baby, sleep.

Sleep, baby, sleep,
Our cottage vale is deep;
The little lamb is on the green,
With woolly fleece so soft and clean—
Sleep, baby, sleep.

Sleep, baby, sleep,
Down where the woodbines creep;
Be always like the lamb so mild,
A kind and sweet and gentle child,
Sleep, baby, sleep.

Hush, Little Baby

Hush, little baby, don't say a word,
Papa's going to buy you a mockingbird.

If that mockingbird won't sing,
Papa's going to buy you a diamond ring.

If that diamond ring turns brass,
Papa's going to buy you a looking glass.

If that looking glass gets broke,
Papa's going to buy you a billy goat.

If the billy goat runs away,
Papa's going to buy you another today.

Little Boy Blue

Little Boy Blue, come blow your horn,

The cow's in the meadow, the sheep in the corn.

But where is the little boy tending the sheep?

He's under the haystack fast asleep.

Will you wake him? No, not I,

For if I do, he's sure to cry.

Rock-a-bye, Baby

Rock-a-bye, baby, on the treetop,

When the wind blows the cradle will rock;

When the bough breaks the cradle will fall,

Down will come baby, cradle, and all.

Glossary

bedbug – a wingless bug that lives in bedding.

bough – a main branch of a tree.

cock – an adult male chicken.

doth – an old way of saying *do*.

fleece – the wool coat of an animal, such as a sheep.

halfpenny roll – a piece of bread that only cost a halfpenny. A halfpenny was a British coin that was valued at half of the new penny.

playfellows – other children to play with.

snoring – to make a loud noise while sleeping.

trousers – another word for pants.

vale – a valley with a stream.

woodbine – a type of honeysuckle.

Web Sites

To learn more about nursery rhymes, visit ABDO Group online at **www.abdopublishing.com**. Web sites about nursery rhymes are featured on our Book Links page. These links are routinely monitored and updated to provide the most current information available.

Ł BEDTI   HROBP
Bedtime with Mother Goose /

ROBINSON
05/11